THE IR

Colby Smith was born and raised in south-ern West Virginia and is currently based in Cleveland, Ohio. His fiction has been pub-lished in numerous anthologies associated with the Neo-Decadent art movement and his non-fiction has appeared in *Vastarien*, *Spontaneous Poetics*, and *The Aither*. His debut short story collection, *The Universe as Performance Art*, is forthcoming from Eibonvale Press.

SNUGGLY BOOKS

colby smith

THE IRONIC SKELETONS

THIS IS A SNUGGLY BOOK

Copyright © 2022 by Colby Smith.
All rights reserved.

ISBN: 978-1-943813-95-7

For MRD.

THE IRONIC SKELETONS

"The mind is its own place, and in itself
Can make a Heav'n of Hell, or a Hell of
Heav'n."
—*Paradise Lost,* Book I, 254-255

"Earth covers Earth
Time tryeth truth."
—Current 93, "Time Tryeth Truth"

I

After I recovered from my hangover I checked my inbox and got an alert from PaleoWire that there was a new, curious article in *The Journal of Human Evolution*. I read the summary and my interest was piqued. Revising, always revising we are; and with this new article, we shall do it again. The article in question was titled "New Hominid from the Koro Toro Region in Chad." The head author was Bruno Dragobych, affiliated with Charles University in Prague; one of the minor authors I had met at a conference, but she left a nasty impression, so I will not disclose his name or institutional affiliation. This is the same region where the upper mandible of *Australopithecus bahrelgazali* was discovered in 1995 by a team headed by the French paleontologist Michel Brunet. Given this, it is unsurprising that a new hominid has been unearthed in that same locale. The authors described a lower jaw and partial cranium. They estimated the remains to be about 3 million years old. Surprisingly, the authors do not purport the animal to be an australopithecine—a subtribe that encompasses all genera related to *Australopithecus* and *Paranthropus*. Most authors lump in *Ardipithecus*, *Praeanthropus*, and *Kenyanthropus* into this group as well. Based on the cranial dimensions, they concluded that the creature's brain exceeded the range of what we know an australopithecine's brain size could achieve—about 700 cubic centimeters. Moreover, the incisors and canines were larger than those of a typical australopithecine, and the post-canines were smaller. It is curious how, since we became aware of ourselves and started telling stories about how we got here, we have constantly rewritten our past, whether through religious or aesthetic evolution or the development of archaeology and paleontology. We are an arrogant species; the fundamentalists were positive of our beginnings (and, often enough, our eventual demise), but when you lose your faith and stand naked before the jaws of the cosmos, and realize that even the cells in your own body are eclipsed by bacteria, you succumb to a profound humility towards your place in the universe, more so than the believer. This is, of course, presuming that one believes that *humans are not an impressive evolutionary accident*. I say this for a number of reasons. Our anatomy is pathetic. We cannot kill anything with our nails or our teeth. Our abdomen is terribly weak. We had to cheat with technology to get at the top. All we have to call our own is language, which will vanish once we do. Language like sperm, impregnating minds with new ideas, experiences past and future, to say everything and nothing at once while other creatures scarcely have to vocalize to understand. And look where that has gotten us. Many of my fellow atheists have fallen into this trap; I claim that, on this basis alone, they are just as archaic and reactionary as the faithful they despise.

II

I deal with the dead. I am not a mortician or a coroner or a necrophile, do so out of academic rather than sexual interest. I am a graverobber. People often mistake me for an archaeologist, but I work with the corpses of things that died before the first written word, before the first uttered word, before the first thought.

The Bible erred when it placed Words before the creation of the world. The word is a recent evolutionary invention. The language I write this in will become extinct some day, just like the creatures I have dedicated my life to studying.

Babel was built for naught.

I don't know why I am writing this down, or why anyone writes anything down if their memory is to dissolve with time. I do it anyway, because I must be a narcissist like everyone else.

My childhood is a kaleidoscopic blur; it is probably better that way. It is difficult to pinpoint the genesis of my interest in prehistoric life. I just know I was especially young, and when my obsession was born I became exceptionally gifted in the subject. I didn't see Spielberg's film until much later, and it was not good. Spielberg is nothing; his reputation has been cultivated on nostalgia and nothing more. Though even more grossly inaccurate, I preferred films like Honda's *Gojira* and Lourié's *The Beast from 20,000 Fathoms* (my introduction to Ray Harryhausen's remarkable special effects). I remember greatly impressing my elementary school teachers with my knowledge.

After high school, I moved out of my home state of West Virginia. I was sheltered from most of the tragedy of the state. An inland island; bald mountains like scalped gods; denizens like the undead, scurrying as rats from the sun.

I thought Ohio would provide an escape from it all, but if anything it made me homesick.

I attended Ohio University, Athens campus. It is the oldest academic institution in the state, founded in 1804 by Menasseh Cutler and Rufus Putnam. The city was slightly larger than my hometown of Beckley. Much cleaner, too—artificially so. It is one of the poorest cities in the United States for many reasons. The weather was rogue: flash floods were common; spring heat was not uncommon in the middle of winter. The strip of Court Street was dominated by local business, but the occasional chain sprung up. By day it was as bustling as a Nazi rally. At the end of sophomore year, when I moved out of the cramped dormitories and into my own apartment, the street was deserted, as it was summer.

I didn't get out much, so my impression of the city is disjointed and fragmentary.

At first I had majored in biological sciences, but my performance in classes oriented towards that degree was mediocre at best, so I switched to geological sciences. I also tacked on a pale-ontology and English minor. I was a pitiful student. I barely studied and preferred to devote my time to extraneous reading; yet I managed to scrape by, even excel. My professors were invariably amiable, though some of them—especially those allied to the humanities—I found clouded by performative naiveté concerning social matters.

When I obtained my degrees, I went to grad school at the University of Colorado in Denver. The music scene was great, but I soon had to wean myself off of Adderall and cocaine

It was an ideal place to pursue my education, as there were several fossiliferous geological formations relatively close to the campus. It was at the Dry Mesa Quarry—a Jurassic sandstone deposit situated in the middle of the stunning, arborous Uncompahgre National Forest—where I discovered the fragmentary skeleton of a novel Anklylosaurid, which I christened *Pyknosaurus lamberti*. This dinosaur was the subject of my thesis, and my peers were impressed that I would find something so remarkable for someone so inexperienced.

I don't deserve this recognition. The general public only cares about the facts and not the names behind the facts. To that end, I will never be a Mary Anning, a Stephen Jay Gould, a Loren Eiseley, a Jack Horner.

These days I haunt the Carnegie Museum of Natural History in Pittsburgh, working as an assistant in the vertebrate paleontology archives. It is quite difficult and tedious work, but I cannot turn back now. This is my destiny and I must be content.

It was a long day at the museum and it was the eve of the weekend, so I decided to go to the Kitty Empire. It prides itself on being gay-owned and gay-operated. Unlike many gay joints, there is no air of sexual elitism.

A miasma of heat wafted against my face when I entered the establishment; a barrage of light assaulted my senses like the mating ritual of an exotic bird. The DJ—I believe it was DJ Vilify that night—was playing a mix of Top 40 and drum and bass. The floor was congested, so I went to the bar and ordered a margarita. My tolerance was low, so two drinks had me smashed and ready to hit the floor.

I danced readily with a blonde with a galaxy of glitter on her face. I didn't ask for her name, probably out of conscious reluctance.

We went to the women's restroom. The bass rattled the room lit with a pseudoinfrared haze. I sank to my knees and pulled her panties to her ankles.

She threw her head back and groaned. Just then I noticed the gold band on her finger.[1]

----

1 "A New Genus of Trilobite Discovered in the Triassic Hosselkus Limestone Calls Into Question the Extent of the P-Tr Extinction Event" had been fermenting in the hands of the editors of *Nature* for eight months. It had yet to see publication. The delay was inexplicable. They had made the proper revisions, and this was a landmark find in our field. Any reasonable editor of a journal would rush to have it published. They emailed the editorial desk numerous times about their procrastination. Most attempts they were ignored, but others they received various response patterns. One was a courteous apology for the delay; that they intake thousands of articles and the order in which they are published is under careful consideration each issue; that their article

※

I called a cab to take me back to my apartment, purged the contents of my enjoyment almost immediately upon entering, prepared a damp washcloth and put it on my forehead.

Just when I was about to sleep, my phone hummed. It was a text message from my colleague Vincent Rosenbaum, allied with the University of Pittsburgh's geology department. We are agreeable acquaintances, and he frequently collaborates with the museum.

2:30 a.m.
VINCENT ROSENBAUM
Hey, D. Sarah and the team just

---

will see print soon. Another was that the article still needs revision, despite it being accepted ages ago. Sometimes they said they had not received an article by that title at all. Frustrated beyond articulation, Sarah proposed that the paper be withdrawn. The other authors declined the proposal. Patience is a virtue, Victor told Sarah. But the money? The recognition? The fruit of patience, Victor reiterated.

came back from Cali and brought back some very unusual stuff. You might be interested in taking a look. Can we come by on Monday?

2:34
ME
Sure, what kind of stuff is it?

2:38
VINCENT ROSENBAUM
At least one of them will completely shake the field. I'm excited for you to see it.

III

I couldn't sleep that night.[1]

Why they would want to show me first, I don't know. I don't specialize in invertebrates,

1 They finished the first draft of their paper, titled "A New Genus of Trilobite Discovered in the Triassic Hosselkus Limestone Calls Into Question the Extent of the P-Tr Extinction Event." They peddled it around to several journals, and after several revisions it was finally accepted by *Nature*. Scarcely any outlet is more prestigious. The bastion of biology–it has published landmark papers on the structure of DNA, the first cloned mammal, the structure of myoglobin, the genome. It has also published the first papers on plate tectonics, the neutron, and the puncture in the ozone. It was, to surrender to my arrogance, an appropriate venue. And what should become of them, having submitted to *Nature*? And what should become of me, having submitted to nature? They shall get prestige in our circles, I shall linger on the periphery. I will never be able to top *Pyknosaurus*. They'll probably split the Paleontological Society Medal. Our Nobel.

and though I recognize their importance in the biosphere—the sheer quantity of species absurdly dwarfs that of vertebrates, my specialty—I have next to no interest in them as a scholar. I suppose my hallucinations punish me for my indifference, for they tend to exhibit an insectoid motif.

Even so, I was profoundly excited and disturbed by what they brought back.

The team was initially looking for remains of ichthyosaurs in the Triassic Hosselkus Limestone. Sarah tells me she was scanning the pallid cliffs for a glimpse of fossils. She had failed to find anything for hours, until a dark spot wedged in the middle of a bed arrested her attention.

She hacked away with her pick with care and precision. When the fossil was free from its prison, she innocently brought it back to the rest of the research team. When they saw what it was, they stood aghast.

It was a trilobite.

I couldn't tell you the genus, but it looked quite generic. Sarah asserts she found it in Hosselkus Limestone and not some other, older deposit. The relative age raised eyebrows, but a few weeks after Vincent and Sarah showed me the specimen, it was radiometrically dated, and it was, indeed, of Triassic age.

It was a fossil that, frankly, should not have existed.

Its implausibility derives from the fact that all genera of trilobite were eradicated during the Permian-Triassic mass extinction—affectionately known by laymen as The Great Dying. It was, of course, the planet's most dramatic extinction event, in which over 90% of all life died. Marine invertebrates, like trilobites, suffered the greatest casualties. There was likely a complex chain of catastrophes that led to the near-decimation of life, from the eruption of the Siberian Traps to the methane-hydrate gasification to the formation of the supercontinent Pangea.

Methodological naturalism, the foundational framework of the scientific method, is, as its name suggests, applied naturalistic philosophy. Naturalism is the idea that there is nature and only nature—that there are no supernatural phenomena. By definition, the supernatural cannot exist in a naturalist system, since nature would be all that exists and there would be no such thing as an "outside" to the system. That being said, most paleontologists are religious on some level, and see little contradiction in their faithful convictions and their work. They are no fundamentalists, but some are certainly devout.

I am not one of those religious scientists.

Nor will I ever be.

IV

I stuck my head in the middle of a campfire and my skull melted like marshmallows.

When I hung myself, the rope bounced like a bungee, and I was still alive shouting WHEEEEEEEE.

I went deaf from the sound of turning pages.

I was lost in a grove.

There was a woman on a pedestal, transversely bisected and still bloody.

I approached the pedestal and she latched on to me, then ate my face.

LED bumblebees making a hive of factories.

Ravegirls vomiting honey.

A presidential orgy of centuries.

The wolf ghost from my childhood licking my privates.

Elephants with radioactive eyes.

Falling towards the moon.

Exercise ad infinitum.

A little boy with slashed arms begging me to kiss him.

An octopus raped a woman to death.

I became a manticore and stung myself.

Incest incest incest.

A circus of harpies.

Lovers performing female circumcision.

The death of music.

Plastic takeover.

Being violated in my sleep.

Liberating a zoo as if it were a concentration camp.

The death of a dog.

The dog resurrected, playing with its exposed organs.

Myself playing with the dog.

The dog rimming me.

The dog whispering sweet nothings in my ear.

Bass crushing rocks.

Treble rending sky.

Songs from my childhood that I have forgotten.

An infant's penis.

Fucking among the crops.

Chickens searching for their heads.

Crippled Indians breaking into the apartment.

Writing a story called "Pony".

Myself as gravestone.

Myself as ash.

V

The following day I had lunch in the cafeteria, as usual. Being an employee, I ate for free; the food is delectable for a museum, so I exploited this discount daily. Switching from fast food to this, I lost about thirty pounds in three months, accompanied by semi-regular exercise.

The person I had lunch with was Garrett Young. He specialized in fossil primates, particularly in the family *Adapidae* (Eocene precursors to lemurs and lorises). A bodybuilder in his spare time, he was built like Mishima in his later years, and had his gapped smile, too. His irises were like coprolites, and his hair the hue of walnuts.

He had a hamburger and a salad. I had the lemon chicken breast with mango salad.

"Some shit about the mass killings in Portugal following the strike."

"I know, fucking monsters."

"You know I'm more to the right than you, but I know brutality when I see it."

"Yeah."

We chewed for a while. I overheard an Arab family talk about the contents of the museum being evil to their children.

"So what did you make of that article I sent you, Garrett?"

"What article?"

"The one in *The Journal of Human Evolution*."

"I never received any sort of email like that."

"Huh, strange. I know it's not quite your area, but thought you'd find it interesting nonetheless."

"Yeah, any news about human evolution should be of interest to anyone. I know you're not particularly concerned with human affairs—"

"The humans we're concerned with were innocent. Before the State, before religion, before agriculture."

"Don't tell me you're an anarcho-primitivist."
"No. Just a misanthrope."
The Arab children were starting to cry.

VI

I ran into Garrett again two days later. He still hadn't received the email. I looked on my mobile phone and showed him where I had sent it.

"Huh, it doesn't look like you sent it at all."

"What? It's right here?"

"No, it isn't. Look."

"I swear to you, it's there."

"How about you send it again?"

"Fine, I'll do it. See if you get a notification on your phone."

"Alright."

I dug up the link, copied it to the clipboard, and sent it to Garrett.

No notification appeared on Garrett's phone.

"Well, that's odd. Could be the connection."

"Yeah, maybe."

The connection was fine.

"Perhaps I'll get it later. I might ask some of my colleagues about it after a while. What did it describe?"

"Oh, some new Pliocene hominid in Chad. It wasn't an australopithecine. I'm not sure exactly what it is."

"Some freak aberration, maybe."

"They didn't go into the phylogenetic implications of the fossil. Surely there's more work to be done before they can conclude anything."

"Yes. Well, I have to get back to work."

"Alright. See you."

A week passed. We were texting about random happenings in the world when I asked him whether or not he got the email. No, he said. Strange, indeed. I asked him what his colleagues thought about the paper.

He said that they had no idea what he was talking about.

VII

I was stopped in the back room by Helen Treadway. She, like Garrett, specialized in early primates. Helen was eaten alive by age, but this did not inhibit her from doing her job well.

"Good morning, D.W."

"Morning, Helen."

"Garrett told me about that new hominid paper and I swear I can't find anything on it. Do you know the volume and issue number?"

"No, sorry. It's the strangest thing, Helen. First that, now the thing with Victor and them."

"Hell, I don't know. I don't suppose it matters."

"It does to me."

"Well, that's your business. Anyway, I've been digging around in this room and I found something that may be of interest to you."

"Yeah?"

"I'll show you."

We walked over to section BF-675. It was directly below the air vent, and we visibly shivered when the torrent of wind poured down on us. I cranked the four-pronged handle and the cabinets spread apart.

"It's over here."

She withdrew a drawer and picked up a small fossil from within. I don't remember the catalogue number.

"Looks like a phalange."

"Yes, that's what I think as well. From a primate or primate-like creature."

"I see."

"So this thing was found in 1886 over at Hell Creek and was mislabelled as a mouse femur."

"Nice, so this could be something like *Purgatorius*?"

"Precisely."

It's always exciting to discover something new in the back catalogue. It is as wondrous as finding a new disease in your body, or finding insects skittering on your kitchen floor when you clean and apply pesticides regularly.

"Have you talked to the director about it?"

"Not yet. I want to be sure I'm correct about this being a new species before I make any moves."

"Seems irresponsible and seedy."

"Well, you're probably right. I'll notify him tomorrow."

"Good. My shift's over in a bit."

"Mine, too. I may stay here overnight, though. Comparing other specimens and what-not."

"Lambert!"

Treadway stopped me in the Hall of African Wildlife. It is one of the more popular exhibits aside from Dinosaurs in their Time, as animals famous and obscure are represented in the bustling savannah scenes frozen in time by taxidermy.

We were by the giant sable antelope. She spoke in an excited hush, so as not to disturb the museum-goers.

"What is it Treadway?"

"It's gone! The phalange is gone!"

"What? Are you sure?"

"Yes, positive!"

We entered the back room and, sure enough, the fossil had vanished.

"Alert the director about this."

"Already have."

"Could someone have stolen it?"

"I don't see what anyone would want with something like that. It's not a particularly spectacular specimen. But your guess as to what happened to it are as good as mine."

The director never took any executive action regarding the primate phalange. When Helen pressed him about it, he rejected her hypothesis of ever having made any sort of grievance to him.

6:45
ME
Want to go clubbing?

6:46
VINCENT ROSENBAUM
I'm happily married and I'm busy.

6:46
ME
Lol okay.

6:47
ME
Still waiting?

6:52
VINCENT ROSENBAUM
On what?

6:54
ME
The paper.

6:57
VINCENT ROSENBAUM
I beg your pardon?

7:00
ME
The paper you wrote with Sarah
and them?

7:05
VINCENT ROSENBAUM
I don't know what you're talking
about.

7:07
ME
You're fucking kidding me.

7:08
ME
You've been hassling Nature for
months about it.

7:09
ME
The goddamn trilobite?

7:10
VINCENT ROSENBAUM
You're crazy. Sarah and I haven't written any paper. Let alone heard anything about a trilobite.

7:14
ME
I don't know what kind of game you're playing, but stop it. You were so worked up over that fucking trilobite that you showed it to me first, even though I know fuck-all about invertebrates. It was Triassic. Found in Triassic limestone and confirmed by absolute age dating.

7:25
VINCENT ROSENBAUM
Fuck you. Something like that

simply wouldn't exist and you know it. If anyone's playing games here it's you.

7:30
ME
Well, fuck you, too, then. I'm not crazy. I saw it.

He didn't respond after that.
Coward.
Cunt.

VIII

It was coming back, my distrust of things. Was this the Spectacle at work? Yea, ionized awareness, straight-edge psychonaut. The corn is dead, long live the corn. The corn is Joan of Arc, or Joan of Arc is the corn, burned but immortal. Snow in summer. The cunt of the virgin is sewn up so vampires will not drain her blood and make her their slave. I laid down, twitching like a junky. I was overcome with an implacable sensation that was at the same time not a sensation at all. Cryptonausea, if you will. I tried throwing up on my own but I couldn't, so I purged into the sink. The cryptonausea remained. My will to go to therapy was that of a mule's. For once I sympathize with those cases of people going through with cannibalism pacts. I thought about performing one with Josh. It wasn't sexual, but rather metaphysical. I wanted to be recycled. Maybe my soul will be recycled into something greater or something lesser than my present self. The Hindus and the Buddhists know it. My transgressions are great. Existing is my greatest transgression.

In my mind I ran through what I could become:

1. A monarch.
2. A bum.
3. A grasshopper.
4. A sex doll.
5. An earwig.
6. An elm.
7. An elephant.
8. A black metal musician.
9. An infant infected with mumps or whooping cough.
10. A gigolo.
11. A clown.
12. An executive.
13. A prostitute.

14. A serial killer.
15. A great author.
16. A messiah.

I blanked. I have a pitiful imagination.

IX

It was a good thing that I had counseling scheduled for the following week. I remember when I saw my first mental health professional in college after a decade or so of neglect. My mother never saw it fit to refer me to one as a child, even though I had displayed anomalous and outright disturbing behavioral patterns. She had assumed that these problems were situational, that they would be overturned with time or better circumstances at school; little did she know. Really, she should have known better, considering that she had a background in mental health. This has come up numerous times in counseling and therapy. I don't know if I'll ever get over it. Anyway, the first. I forget his name; probably stamped it out from my mind as soon as I left the office. He was an Indian man with a thin, fox-like face. In his office was an array of houseplants, a shelf stuffed with books like *The Gift of Therapy*, and a little gold Buddha complementing the pictures of his children riding an Asian elephant on his desk.

It is strange that I remember so much minutiae, but not his name.

He welcomed me, exchanged psychological formalities.

What seems to be the problem?

What purpose do you have in life?

What do you do to keep these thoughts away?

Do you have a family history?

Do you take drugs?

Do you feel like you are in immediate danger of hurting yourself?

What are the voices telling you?

What do you see?

What makes you think you have x disorder?

And so on.

I explained what was wrong with me in graphic detail. I couldn't do anything to keep those thoughts away. I did have a family history, on both my parents' sides; mostly depression of some sort. I didn't take nearly as much drugs as I do now. I had barely experimented with marijuana and acid by then. I was a fledgling. I didn't feel like I was in any immediate danger of hurting myself, but I did have a master plan gestating for years that no amount of therapy could sever me from. On my 50th birthday, I will overdose. I had read some Mishima by then and had developed a morbid fascination for his character. His primary motivation for bodybuilding was not so that he could have a Hellenic figure for the sake of it, but rather to stave off the decay of the body. I am in my mid-thirties now, and I anticipate my final day more than I did when I was younger.

I'd always found suicide an aesthetically gratifying way to go.

The voices were telling me that there was a grand conspiracy, especially in the leftist circles at the university, to murder me. Utter strangers were in on it. When they made eye contact with me on the street I wondered what they knew about me. They knew something, or else they wouldn't be interested enough to stare me down like a matador stares down a bull in the ring. They were also telling me to kill myself and kill others. It is a wonder that I did not become a school shooter. I had masturbated to thoughts of Dylan Klebold penetrating my asshole, and I seriously considered purchasing an Eric Harris-inspired NATURAL SELECTION shirt from the Internet. In those days I wanted to commit arson against people involved in social justice circles, who had wronged me because I was more than a little politically incorrect. I saw things I care not to describe. I dreamt worse things. I reckoned I had X disorder because my friends who majored in psychology said that my symptoms resembled X disorder. I told him everything I could within the 30 minutes I had with him—and I was very explicit with him—but he told me what was wrong with me on my behalf. I had not felt so alone until that moment. The appeal of suicide for me is that it seems to defy nature. We are so used to involuntary stimuli, either in the internal or external environment, causing death. Suicide, on the other hand, is a voluntary fatal stimulus. There are rumors that several other animals do this, but we know of only one for sure. Ants have the capacity to self-destruct, showering a predator with noxious slime to preserve the colony in arthropod jihad. *Kamikaze* pilots and suicide bombers could be considered human ants. Religious objections to suicide, as Schopenhauer demonstrated in his essay on the subject, have no grounds on which to base their grievance. No Biblical edict forbids it. Samson exterminated himself by forcing pillars of the Philistine temple to collapse on his head. And what was the Crucifixion on lonely Golgotha but an assisted suicide? Hume also points out that suicide does not necessarily violate the will of God; for if God demanded that we enjoy life, and that all events are predestined, then it is inevitable that the suicide go through with the act, and it is only right that they do so to service their happiness. As religion is known for being an anchor to human autonomy, it is predictable that it should attempt to restrict the greatest expression of human autonomy ever conceived by the imagination. Suicide is anatomical anarchy. Suicide is also closely tied to art. Numerous depictions of antique suicides exist, notably Lucretia and Sappho. The plays of Shakespeare are rife with the act. Often before committing *seppuku*, a samurai would compose a poem commemorating his death. And what of all the writers, musicians, and artists who have done it? There are studies that purport that creative people are more susceptible to debilitating mental illness than non-creative people. Would the romance of Antony and Cleopatra have been as notable if the monarch and politician were slaughtered by those under the wings of the Roman eagle rather than asp-fangs and gladius guided by their own hands? What artistry might Nero have declared if he had died from some common plague of his time? Would the practice of *seppuku* retain its signature philosophy of atonement if the transgressor was murdered by those he did wrong against rather than by he, himself, who committed the wrong? Martyrs are content with dying for their causes; indeed, most aggressively seek death to endorse them! But one must be careful not to prioritize romanticism over practicality in one's results.

Eating houseplants is not as effective as eating pills.

Cutting yourself with a butter knife is not as effective as cutting yourself with a hunting knife.

Smothering yourself with a blanket is not as effective as smothering yourself with natural gas from your stove.

In a viciously authoritarian existence, where even libertines are expected to follow laws out of decency or obligation, there are few choices we can truly call our own. Even our choice to abstain or indulge in drugs is partially governed by genetic predisposition, as I can attest. The subject of free will is a moot point. I am agnostic on its existence. Counselors and peers keep us alive, fattening us, stimulating us with joy, only to prolong the eventual slaughter to come. No man fears anything more than death, the Big Black, the Cessation.

X

My current therapist is an old, fat dyke named Shannon. I do not mean to insult her by calling her a dyke, for she dons the label with pride. I am allowed to call her a dyke anyways, since I am a half-dyke.

I checked myself in at the front desk and sat in the waiting room. Populated by disturbed old men and women; I could tell more disturbed than myself just by looking at them. I wondered if it got worse with age or if I am just striking poses with my mind. I discussed the latter point with Shannon once. She said that everyone's struggles are valid, and that I shouldn't think of myself as a psychological poseur because a) I have explicit symptoms b) these symptoms can be treated with medication c) I wouldn't be in that room if I were feigning it all. Sorry, Shannon, I said, but that is bullshit. Why? Well, I have known, in my teenage years, spoiled degenerate girls who attempted suicide after their cell phones were confiscated by their parents; that is an inhuman motivation, because it demonstrates that technological malnourishment can be fatal, and this is a sign of weakness in our culture; this is probably my only conservative position.

She agreed.

I noticed that there were more children in the waiting room. They minded their own business well enough despite being tormented by mental illness (presumably why they were there, could easily have been behavioral problems unrelated to any kind of psychosis; after all, the facility was both a mental health and behavioral center). They are perhaps stronger than adults suffering from debilitating mental conditions since:

1. Lack of financial and occupational responsibility.

2. Surviving despite lack of cognitive and emotional intelligence found in adults.

3. Suicide is actively kept secret from children.

I flipped through a book to pass the time. I cannot remember what title it was.

A woman stumbled in front of me.

There was no television in the waiting room. The sound of the air vents was oppressive, like a windstorm howling through a desert.

Shannon opened the door on the right side of the room and called my name twice, for I didn't hear her the first time.

She led me back to her office, the end of a labyrinth. She bade me to sit down in either of the two leather chairs; I took my usual spot, because the seat in the other one had a tear in it and it annoyed me. Children's drawings were tacked to the wall, presented with as much reverence as a major painting hung in a prestigious gallery.

"How are you doing?"

"You won't believe me if I said I was fine. You never do."

She logged onto her desktop computer. The

operating system was outdated. She started to type.

The sound of typing hurt my ears.

"What's going on?"

"Well, a lot."

"Tell me about it."

"The incest dreams are getting worse and more frequent."

"I'm sorry. How are they getting worse?"

"It was just with my mom at first. Then with my dad. Sometimes both at once. Now my little brother is getting in the picture."

She typed.

I teared up. I usually didn't show any emotion this early in the interview, if any at all.

"It's okay."

"No, it isn't."

"Would you like a change in your medication today?"

"No."

"Why not?"

"I just don't."

"But you just said that the incest dreams are getting worse."

She typed some more. I talked.

". . . I got home from work the other day and I saw the fireflies in broad daylight again. I went straight to my room and started thinking about the time I was raped. I didn't flinch or cry or anything . . . my struggle. I reached for my pocket knife on the nightstand and started to tease my thighs with the blade. I drew blood."

She kept her mitts away from the keyboard. The silence was overpowering.

"Anything else been going on?"

"It involves my work, so I can't really tell you, but I think I'm starting to process things that aren't really there. More extreme than usual. For instance, I ask someone about something I saw in the news, and they have no idea what I'm talking about. I'm thinking about getting a gun now that open-carry is legally acceptable in this state."

Her eyes tore at my soul like a vulture tears at a carcass. She hadn't done this even when I had threatened suicide.

XI

I got back to the apartment, watched *Accattone* (1961, dir. Pier Paolo Pasolini). A relatively tame debut compared to some of his other films, namely *Porcile* (1969) and *Salò, or the 120 Days of Sodom* (1975), I could understand why an Italian audience would be simultaneously scandalized and moved by its frank depiction of Roman slum life and how Pasolini forces the audience to sympathize with the titular anti-hero. I devoured copious amounts of popcorn, pausing the film often just to pace around the room, even to go to the grocery store just to purchase more food. It took me four, perhaps five hours to finish the film. I slept for sixteen hours; it was the weekend, and I couldn't afford this kind of sleep on weekdays. I would surely miss work, and though I have decent standing at the museum my position is, like all positions, expendable.

I sieved the paleontological news from the tedious global events on my feed. Against my nature, I went to a potentially tabloid popular science website, where I found a rather curious article detailing a find by UC Berkeley. In an unspecified cave, the remains of a *bird with teeth* were discovered, and were evidently young enough to be C14 dated. I was skeptical of this, of course, as pelagornithids vanished with the dinosaurs at the K-T boundary. However, there was a proper journal citation at the end of the article, and a link to a press release from the university. I was relieved.

I bookmarked it for future reference and went to sleep.

The following day two men—let's call them Josh and Dennis—arranged a threesome with me at one of their houses. I believe it was Josh's. Perhaps they were roommates, I don't recall. They were childhood friends; Josh worked in accounting and Dennis worked for a budding tech company that, I'm fairly certain, went under, and last time I talked to Dennis he had been looking for a new job. Josh was slightly muscular, hair red as the skin of a Siamese fighting fish, 16 mm gauges, an array of tattoos from kanji to tigers, and had a healthy exposure to childhood trauma. Dennis was fat, hairy, bespectacled, skin devoid of modifications. Both wore band shirts and tight jeans often.

Sex is a combat sport. Your partner is your enemy, no matter how close you are emotionally or what sexual dynamic you have. Sacred/profane, sacred + profane?

The work-day was long and uneventful. Even the weather was unremarkable.

When I returned home I read a typical paper for once. It described a new Oligocene lagomorph from Wyoming. Taxonomic relation unspeculated. I am not especially interested in lagomorphs unless they are gravy. The following day I brought up the paper to some colleagues and they actually acknowledged its existence. A boulder had been lifted off my shoulders.

I slept more soundly than I had in some time. I don't remember any remarkable dreams, which is comforting, as my dreams are usually bothersome.

A couple weeks later I went through my bookmarks. I remembered the Pleistocene toothed bird article from that popular science website. I clicked on the link, and, lo! there it was unmolested. I read through the article again. Unchanged, from what I recall. I scrolled to the bottom of the article and clicked the article source.

404 not found.

Are you fucking kidding me? I said aloud.

I backtracked.

The original article was gone.

XII

a. Therefore I am losing my mind.

b. Therefore there is a conspiracy against me at the museum.

c. Therefore I was wrong and there is a God and He is toying with me. Perhaps Satan? A demiurge?

d. Therefore these fossils are not real.

e. Therefore these fossils are real.

f. Therefore we know everything.

g. Therefore we know nothing.

h. Therefore the present is the key to the past.

i. Therefore the present is not the key to the past.

j. Therefore the past is key to the present.

k. Therefore the past is not key to the present.

l. Therefore the honeymoon of insanity and reality.

m. Therefore the death of reason.
n. Therefore the inclusion of hallucination into objective perception.
o. Therefore what God could it be?
p. Therefore which religion is right?
q. Therefore which religion is wrong?
r. Therefore the sun goes out.
s. Therefore the moon goes in.
t. Therefore the crowned prince of the Earth shall sow the seeds of perceptual discord.
u. Therefore the soul is a parasite.
v. Therefore hexagrammatical figures which blur overtop each other in the most occult texts become legible as ternary diagram.
w. Therefore the rocks lie.
x. Therefore what can be called history in the rocks?
y. Therefore the light contracts.
z. Therefore the screen is going out.

XIII

(D.W. *and* VINCENT *sitting at a cafeteria table eating chicken and rice, packed with protein and carbohydrates. Center stage lit.*)

D.W.: Hey Jude, don't make it bad.

VINCENT: Fucking hell.

D.W.: So, am I pregnant?

VINCENT: You tell me.

D.W.: No.

VINCENT: Why?

D.W.: I asked you. It was a command.

VINCENT: But how should I know?

D.W.: 50/50 probability.

VINCENT: Then yes.

D.W.: No.

VINCENT: Why not?

D.W.: Have you read Schopenhauer?

VINCENT: That is selfish.

D.W.: It is selfless.

VINCENT: You're like an atheist dismissing religion.

D.W.: That, too.

VINCENT: I wish I were a homosexual.

D.W.: Why?

VINCENT: Fuck women.

D.W.: I do.

VINCENT: Marriage?

D.W.: Till death.

(They fuck on the table, smearing the food on each other. VINCENT cums inside D.W. After they finish, D.W. slaps VINCENT across the face.)

VINCENT: Why did you do that?

D.W.: Do what thou wilt shall be the whole of the Law.

VINCENT: Solipsism.

D.W.: And what have you done?

VINCENT: I was born. That is all.

D.W.: And then?

VINCENT: That is all.

D.W.: I have done more than be born.

VINCENT: No, you haven't.

D.W.: We are paleontologists.

VINCENT: Not philosophers.

D.W.: Natural philosophers, perhaps.

VINCENT: Unnatural philosophers, certainly not.

D.W.: No, I'm a librarian.

VINCENT: A bricklayer.

D.W.: A steelworker.

VINCENT: A police officer.

D.W.: A ditch-digger.

VINCENT: A mortician.

D.W.: A soldier.

VINCENT: A slave driver.

D.W.: An architect.

VINCENT: An engineer.

D.W.: A postwoman.

VINCENT: Post-woman.

D.W.: Androgyny?

VINCENT: Beyond androgyny.

D.W.: It's my birthday today.

VINCENT: Happy birthday.

D.W.: No thank you.

(A birthday cake manifests on the table. D.W. gorges herself on the cake then purges it back up again.)

VINCENT: You are such an empty being.

D.W.: Especially now.

VINCENT: Clean up the vomit.

D.W.: I'll leave it for the crows.

(*Enter* GARRETT YOUNG *and* HELEN TREADWAY.)

GARRETT: Good morning.

HELEN: Good morning.

D.W.: Good afternoon.

VINCENT: Good evening.

GARRETT: What are you doing?

D.W.: What are *you* doing?

HELEN: We were discussing a new dinosaur.

VINCENT: What dinosaur is new?

GARRETT: None of them.

VINCENT: What is it?

HELEN: Something that could only be described as ironic.

D.W.: Ironic, you say, instead of, perhaps, idiosyncratic?

GARRETT: Yes.

HELEN: Well, both.

VINCENT: Well, what warrants that word instead of the other?

HELEN: Do you recall *Chilesaurus*?

D.W.: Yes.

VINCENT: Yes.

GARRETT: Worse than that.

D.W.: In what way?

GARRETT: Paleontological platypus.

VINCENT: But worse than *Chilesaurus*?

D.W.: Carnivorous sauropod?

GARRETT: Right track.

D.W.: What of the hip? Saurischian or ornithischian?

HELEN: Both.

GARRETT: Neither.

VINCENT: But a dinosaur.

D.W.: Not a dinosaur?

HELEN: Yes.

GARRETT: Yes.

D.W.: Neither, but a dinosaur.

GARRETT: Yes.

HELEN: Yes.

(D.W. *pulls a pen out of her vagina and takes notes on her flesh.*)

D.W.: Go on.

GARRETT: The illium midways between short and long.

HELEN: The acetabulum oval-shaped.

GARRETT: The pubis hanging neither forward nor backward. Midways.

HELEN: And the teeth indicate an omnivorous diet.

GARRETT: And it has the claws of a therizinosaur.

HELEN: And the neck of a sauropod.

GARRETT: And the hide of a thyreophoran.

(D.W. *writes, filling her left arm with notes Then her right leg. Then her belly.*)

D.W.: I should get these notes tattooed on me.

VINCENT: Yes.

GARRETT: Will you forget them if you do not tattoo them on yourself?

HELEN: I reckon she will forget even if they were tattooed onto her flesh.

GARRETT: It is nice flesh, akin to a lamb when it is sheared.

HELEN: Yes.

D.W.: Even with these notes?

GARRETT: We will make you forget.

(GARRETT *fetches a bucket of cleaning solution. He splashes it on* D.W.'s *body and the notes fade and slither off her flesh.*)

HELEN: There.

D.W.: Why did you do that?

GARRETT: You must forget.

D.W.: How can I forget an ironic dinosaur?

GARRETT: You must.

HELEN: The human present is more important than the inhuman past.

GARRETT: What effect do things that happened millions or billions or trillions of years ago have on you now, D.W.?

D.W.: That is my life. That is my income. That is my only love.

HELEN: This amounts to nothing.

GARRETT: All life is fleeting.

HELEN: All income temporary.

GARRETT: All love fruitless.

(HELEN *hands* D.W. *a knife.*)

HELEN: Use this.

GARRETT: Against yourself.

HELEN: Against your body.

GARRETT: Against your soul.

D.W.: No.

GARRETT: I don't mean to kill yourself.

HELEN: No, don't kill yourself.

GARRETT: We need you, D.W.

HELEN: Yes, we need you.

GARRETT: We want you, too.

HELEN: Yes, we want you.

GARRETT: Cut off a piece of your flesh.

HELEN: Doesn't matter where.

GARRETT: Could be the flap of your elbow.

HELEN: Or a bit of your heel.

GARRETT: Or a slice of your buttocks.

HELEN: Or a slice of your belly.

GARRETT: It doesn't matter.

(D.W. *obeys. She chooses the flap of her elbow. She doesn't scream or flinch.* HELEN *and* GARRETT *split the piece of flesh and eat it.*)

HELEN: The lamb bleats.

GARRETT: The eucharist.

HELEN: The flesh has turned into bread.

(D.W. *brandishes the knife and approaches* JOSH.)

JOSH: I have a right to life.

D.W.: By what authority?

JOSH: God's.

D.W.: You may have a right to life but you have a sentence to death.

JOSH: The right for it to be long and happy.

D.W.: No life is happy.

JOSH: Why?

D.W.: God willed you and me and everyone else to suffer.

JOSH: That was the fault of Eve.

D.W.: No.

JOSH: That was the fault of you.

D.W.: No.

JOSH: Eve is not mitochondrial.

D.W.: Yes She is.

JOSH: Eve is literal. She was deceived by Lucifer.

D.W.: Lucifer is the light.

(D.W. *stabs* JOSH *numerous times. He dies. She skins him.*)

Blackout.

XIV

I was about to go into the field for the first time in what seemed like aeons. I had been so accustomed to working in a sterile microclimate that I had forgotten what it meant to get filthy outdoors. My lifestyle was practically sedentary by then so I was ill-prepared.

I took the initiative to get back into shape, if not severely. I was never good at working out. Female bodybuilders confused me; they were objects of envy. I did enough to get by. I cut out the junk significantly, but not entirely. I still drank but infrequently. I got advice from my physician, a personal trainer, and friends who were heavily into fitness. Immediately after waking up I would eat breakfast (eggs, yogurt, toast), pace around the apartment for a half hour waiting for the food to settle, and then run ten blocks and back. Pittsburgh at 5 a.m. is cold and stark, but not as frightening as it is during the witching hour. I would come back, rest, then go at it again with dumbbells. I owned a set of 10 lb, 20 lb, and 35 lb weights. A friend sold me his weight bench for an agreeable price. I put it in the living room.

My sessions lasted about half an hour after my run. Rows, 10 reps on each arm, 10 lb, then 20 lb, then 35 lb. Shoulder press, 4 sets of 15 reps, 10 lb then 20 lb. After a month of work I could do 5 reps 35 lbs. Curls, 4 sets of 10 reps. Crunches, 2 sets, 50 reps. Etc.

I couldn't bear to go to an actual gym. Gyms are breeding grounds for narcissism and shame. I didn't have the patience for that.

My core and arms became fairly more toned. It was by no means a dream body, but it sufficed.

I gained more confidence in myself.

Sex would probably be better.

Weaponized distortion
Confusion settles
Like sediment at the bottom
Of a lake.

I brought this
Upon myself
Because I was born
And did not remain
In the darkness.

The field expedition was going to take me to Leon County, Florida. Tallahassee, the state capitol, is located here. There are a variety of geological formations in this county. There are Triassic and Jurassic basalts; there is a gap in Cretaceous deposits and goes straight to the Paleocene. Likewise, there is a gap in the Eocene record, and regular chronology begins at the Oligocene epoch. My team—composed of Darrell Parkinson and Ashley Young of the Carnegie Museum of Natural History, Wesley

Smith and Dennis Rogers of U Pitt, and Vinny Shields of Penn State—were most interested in the Early Miocene formations. Two exist: the St. Marks Formation in the southern part of the county, with fossiliferous packstone and wackestone—the only known phylum that is represented by this formation is Mollusca, not very interesting; the Torreya Formation, overlaying the Floridian aquifer and composed of quartz siliciclastics, is much more interesting, yielding an array of paleofauna, especially vertebrates. It was the latter formation that attracted our attention.

I packed my hand-lens, my magnifying glass, my shit-kicking boots (as I affectionately call them), my canteen, my pick, my backpack stuffed with my laptop and other items, protein bars, my sombrero, and other items I cannot place.

It took us two years to get an excavation permit. We couldn't afford to fuck up.

XV

The team met at the museum. I had not met any of these people in person before, except for Young and Parkinson; but there was, of course, preliminary email exchange for planning purposes.[1]

Ashley Young was a postgraduate student who had been at the Museum for a year. Shorter than I was, her hair was an almost artificial blonde, and her eyes were dirty blue. She was not fat but she was not slim either. Her glasses scarcely fit her face. I disliked her falsetto voice and her chipper demeanor was a practical irritant. Her interests were also degenerate:

---

1 Before the Miocene epoch, Florida was a carbonate platform, so no dinosaurs will ever be found in Florida. Fast-forward to the Pleistocene. Leon County was inhabited by Clovis paleoindians, and subsequently usurped by the Archaic culture.

geek culture and gardening were her main obsessions. She specialized in invertebrates. They were not the focus of our dig, but it never hurts to include an invertebrate paleontologist on your team. Most of us can recognize what sort of invertebrate it is when the fossil is discovered, but we would be fucked when it came to describing it, or if it was worth keeping.[1]

Darrell Parkinson (stout, brunet, vaguely handsome, always dressed in a three-piece suit, even when it was summer, for the sake of novelty) was one of my colleagues in the vertebrate paleontology department. He specialized in pachyderms, and was especially interested in the genus *Deinotherium*. The name of the animal comes from the Greek meaning "terrible beast". Consider an elephant, but instead of the tusks

---

1 The first unique culture to take hold in the region was the Deptford culture, a subdivision of the Woodland culture. The Deptford culture, named after the Deptford area near Savannah, was characterized by decorated pottery, mound building, reliance on cultigens, permanent settlements, and heightened political complexity. Lake Miccosukee in Leon County is a notable archaeological site associated with the Deptford culture. Afterwards, the Swift

erupting from beside the mouth, they jutted from the lower jaw and curved downward like scimitars. Generally larger than contemporary elephants as well. They were extant from the Middle Miocene to the Early Pleistocene. No *Deinotherium* have been found in America, but given my streak of encountering inexplicable fossils it would not surprise me if we found one on this dig.[1]

Wesley Smith was a graduate student at U Pitt. He was, for lack of a better phrase, a jock. He told us on the jeep ride down to Florida that he didn't care about minerals or igneous rocks or metamorphic rocks. His primary concern was sedimentary rocks, and only because of the fossils. He didn't even have an active interest in plate tectonics, the unifying theory of geology. I laughed at him internally. Pathetic creature, limiting yourself like that.[2]

---

1 Creek culture appeared, followed by the Weeden Island and Mississippian cultures.

2 The first major contact that Europeans had with Leon County was in 1539. By this time, the traditional Apalachee people had settled in the Florida Panhandle.

Dennis Rogers was more of a nerd or a sissy. He was, unlike Wesley, practically a generalist, and I tolerated him more for it. Dennis had a black bowl cut and horn-rimmed glasses. He was a cliche. Dennis was interested in fossil *Carnivora*.[1]

Vinny Shields was the only university professor accompanying us on the dig. His real name wasn't Vinny, but I don't know what it was. I asked if it was Vincent; he said no. Vinny

---

Conquistador Hernando de Soto brought priests to the Apalachee capital of Anhaica, or modern-day Tallahassee. The Catholicism that they forced on the natives was accompanied by smallpox and conflict, echoing the results of the Aztec and Inca conquests.

1 After a failed native revolt and a few exchanges of governorship between the Spanish and the British, Florida became a United States territory in 1821. Before Tallahassee became the capital, St. Augustine and Pensacola were potential sites. Plantations were founded in Leon County, and by the 1860s the slave economy allowed it to become the wealthiest county in Florida. During the American Civil War, only one battle took place in the county: the Battle of Natural Bridge on March 6th, 1865, a negligible battle. After the cotton industry dissolved, dairy and beef cattle became the chief industry of the county to the present day.

was exceedingly tall. Perhaps he had a genetic disorder. His hair was a gray halo. Though he was an academic, he had an amiable and humble air about him. His specialty was trace fossils.

※

We went in a small caravan. It took us 14 hours to reach our destination. We stayed in a Marriott hotel in Tallahassee on the first night. It cost us nothing, since Vinny travels a lot and offered to use the points he accumulated on his Marriott card. The view was not exceptional, but the amenities compensated for it. I had stayed in plenty of Marriotts before, and this one was not unique. It was distinctly a Marriott, but that was its only outstanding quality. Leaving the hotel at 8 a.m., we ventured to the southern outskirts of Tallahassee, halfway towards Woodville. Tumbling hills and woods dominated the landscape. When I was a child I feared the woods, fearing what might be in the woods. Witches, murderers, mythological beasts. I feared no longer.

We made camp at the base of a massive hill. There was a series of sizeable outcrops a couple miles away. The terrain wasn't treacherous. We would begin operations the following morning. We gathered wood to erect a fire. There was a stream nearby, and Wesley went over to fish. He caught two largemouth bass, one 9 inches tip to tip and the other 13 inches. He clumsily filleted the fish and, when twilight shrouded the hills around us, we cooked and ate them over the fire. The meat was lean and good. Ashley was getting media withdrawal, I conjectured. The U Pitt boys told obscene jokes. Vinny told us stories of his experiences in the field, for the sake of entertainment and to fortify us for tomorrow's work. I listened with great interest. Darrell was silent most of the night.

I dreamt of things in the forest.

Vinny woke us up by banging one of the pots. He brewed dark coffee for us. Ashley couldn't stomach it. The rest of us made do with it.

I had the desire to shower, but not the means.

So is the wilderness.

Wesley and I were sent out for reconnaissance. It took two hours for us to reach the outcrops. We had conversation, but it was unremarkable, fucking negligent in fact. The more I spent time with him, the more I wanted an accident to happen, for my sake and his.

We started to climb the outcrop. The view behind us was marvelous. I could see the camp.

When we got towards the top of the outcrop I nearly lost my grip from shock. Naked before the sun was the fossil of what looked like a centipede, but it covered a significant portion of the outcrop. Larger than *Arthropleura*. This made no sense, for arthropods didn't even get that large in the Carboniferous.

I had a witness this time.

Wesley and I ran back to camp and alerted the others to our find.

"A centipede 5 meters long?" Vinny asked.

"I swear," Wesley said. "God as my witness.

D.W., as well."

"Yes, I saw it. We can lead you to it."

"Well, stranger things have been found. Take us to the outcrop."

We went back, and my heart sank.

The fossil wasn't there.

"Were you drinking?" Vinny scolded us.

"No," both of us refuted.

"So you were lying."

"No, I saw it," Wesley said.

"Two years to get this permit!" Darrell yelled.

"Precious resources!" Dennis echoed.

"Listen," I said, "this has been going on for over a year. I, for some reason, discover fossils, whether firsthand or secondhand, of an inexplicable character, and they are physically and psychically taken away from me, like an orphan from its parents. I assure you I am not insane. I assure you I am earnest. I cannot explain this phenomenon, but why should I? You wouldn't believe me anyways."

"We don't," Vinny said.

"Fine," I replied. "We'll keep looking at the other outcrops. Maybe we missed the one Wesley and I went to."

We found nothing.

Nothing came out of that expedition. Fame, glory, even a measly tooth. I'd not felt more wasted in my entire career.

We made the drive back to Pittsburgh in silence.

XVI

A tsunami of depression came over me. Therapy wouldn't help; I had to ride the tiger, to
borrow Evola's phrase. I am embarrassed to
have even known Evola, but it was inevitable
that I encountered him. I had entered my own
private Kali Yuga. I called in sick often when I
was healthy. I'm sure they would understand if I
told them the truth. No, they wouldn't. Ameri-
cans do not take mental health seriously unless
it is used as a scapegoat to disarm its people. It
is a figment of the imagination until elementary
school children are torn apart by military-grade
bullets. I have been told that, when I was still a
vegetarian, that my shift in diet was to blame
for my depressive episodes. I wanted to kill
the person who told me that. I didn't follow
through, of course. My body started to degen-

erate. I gained 20 lbs. The skin under my arms was starting to become loose; that beneath my eyes became purples alluvial fans; my bones were growing weaker; menstruation was becoming more laborious. I was a character in a black comedy—an instrument of satire. I took up cutting. I got over my fear of the knife. It was not my wisest decision, but it was my own decision.

It was during this period that I found out my brother died. The circumstances were tragic yet darkly hilarious. He was partying and was hazed by his friends. There was alcohol and fentanyl in his system. I found this funny because I interpreted this as him taking after me.

I went to his funeral almost reluctantly. I saw extended family who asked about my profession. One of them asked what good it was to study prehistoric life. I yelled at him and went outside for a cigarette.

It was an open-casket service.

While the pastor delivered his eulogy, I thought about fucking my brother in death. The corpse was taut yet had a tender aura to it. I shouldn't think these thoughts, but I do. This is why I cut myself; I hate my own thoughts and I deserve to be punished for them.

I stayed with my parents for a few days. They told me they had divorced. Cheating, my mother said. Father was staying just for the funeral.

Since they had parted, they were dead, too.

The depression eventually eroded away. I started exercising again and got back on medication. Things were looking up. One thing bothered me, however. I had contacted Wesley about the dig, and he said he didn't remember seeing a centipede.

This cannot go on.

XVII

Why are the dead cold and why are the living warm and why the moon and the sun likewise and why do I paralyze myself as I think such hideous banal thoughts and why is there a blazing blizzard in my sinus cavity and why is all the beer gone and why is all the wine gone and why is all the money gone and why is all the hope gone and why can I not remember the face of the hope's mother and why do I associate hope with my mother when her attempts to instill a foundation of hope in me in hindsight were all for naught and why is it so hard to stop writing and just autoeuthanize myself already I the cowardly cunt the useless cunt that has done nothing and will do nothing and ought not to have been born and why don't I consume alps of that glorious glorious molecule $C17H21NO4$

which neutralizes the milk of insomnia so my
heart can implode inverse lub dub bud bul and
why is etc. also &c. and why was I never allowed
to have pets and why must we piss for bosses like
infants and why must we get beaten for crying
and why are the shells of snails not hollow and
why is the biological presence of the Fibonacci
spiral significant and why does the phylogeny of
the turtles and the tortoises have taxonomists
thrashing like eels and why do they dance like
that together and why do you suppose they will
not go to their respective houses alone and why
do you suppose neither of them will consider
cherishing me as well and why do you suppose
they do not deserve to live for this minor transgression against my person and why is the α of
the black hole unknown and why is the Ω of
the black hole unknown and why have we been
spared the supermassive maw of nihil and why
has Ύπνος abandoned me and why has Άρτεμις
condemned me to life and why do statues shatter but plexiglass does not shatter and why is
Nora a fuckbird and why does the pen bleed
out before its job is done and why do I dream of

nothing sometimes and why do mammals have tits while reptiles utterly lack tits except for the old synapsids which Oftrolal (2002) said lactated and why am I terrified of shaving wet with a straight razor and why am I afraid of cutting south with a straight razor and why am I afraid of cutting across with a straight razor and why am I afraid of fire like some fucking forest and why am I afraid of darkness and why am I afraid of taking too many capsules and why am I afraid of celebrating my evolutionary heritage and jump in a body of water and drink all around me and piss ammonia in pitiful concentrations and why was love what got Ovid banished and why did a mistake get Ovid banished and why did he not disclose the nature of the love and the mistake and why am I irritated by sounds and why am I aroused by other sounds and why don't I ever hit mute and why can't I hear the breath of friends and strangers through this monitor screen and why did Shakespeare write so much and why did Dante write so little and why did Jesus weep and why does the light never go out and why does fruit turn brown and why was Poe betrayed by the cats he loved and why were the casualties of Caligula's War with the Sea so petty and why won't whalewitches wander warily and why must the bad die old and why is my forehead bleeding and why is the washing machine so noisy and why must hornets exist and why must the penis be an object of envy and why must love be divorced from the penis in its purest form and why must the love-penis impale one orifice at once and why must Darwin have eaten such beautiful creatures and why was the United States cursed with an acutely deformed parliament and why are the armored fishes dead and why is the Rapa Nui tongue dead and why is Roma dead and why is *Dinosauria* dead and why are ghost towns dead and why is Walt Disney dead and why are the Huns dead and why are the Mughals dead and why is empire itself dead and why is feudalism dead and why is communism dead and why are my friends dying and why is my family dying and why is the honeybee dying and why is the rhinoceros dying and why is the red panda dying and why is the okapi dying and why is the

jaguar dying and why is the red wolf dying and
why is the hippopotamus dying and why are
the sea turtles dying and why are the sharks dying and why are the tortoises dying and why is
the polar bear and why is the black footed ferret
dying and why are the giraffes dying and why
are the mantids dying and why are the leopards
dying and why is the river dolphin dying and
why are the frogs dying and why are all the other great apes dying and why is the pangolin dying and why are the seals dying and why are the
antelopes dying and why are the whales dying
and why are the penguins dying and why are the
fish dying and why are the tigers dying and why
are the sloths dying and why are the butterflies
dying and why is the axolotl dying and why is
the bandicoot dying and why is the armadillo
dying and why is the chinchilla dying and why
are the civets dying and why are the binturongs
dying and why are the alligators dying and why
are the crocodiles dying and why is the albatross
dying and why are the camels dying and why is
the gray parrot dying and why is the redwood
dying and why is the Komodo dragon dying

and why are the otters dying and why is the orca dying and why are the seahorses dying and why is the mongoose dying and why is the zebra dying and why are the bats dying and why are the tapirs dying and why is the manatee dying and why are the eagles dying and why are the owls dying and why are the hummingbirds dying and why are the lemurs dying and why are the Tasmanian devils dying like their noble kin the thylacine PBUT and why is the Great West dying and why is the Greater East dying and why is writing itself dying O! great Ἑρμῆς and why are the medicines I am taking contributing to my dying and why is music dying and why are all the stars dying and why is space dying and why is time dying and why are You dying and why is the moth fluttering against my window dying and why am I dying and why does anyone do anything at all if they are dying why why why?

GOD: THE DEAD AND THE MOON ARE COLD BECAUSE I WILLED THEM SO AND THE LIVING AND THE SUN ARE WARM BECAUSE I WILLED THEM

SO AND ETC BECAUSE I WILLED
THEM SO AND YOU WILL NOT
QUESTION MY WILL BECAUSE MY
WILL IS GREATER THAN THE WILL
OF MAN FOR THEY ARE SUBJECT TO
MY WILL AS FOR YOUR POSITION
THERE IS SOMETHING FUNDA-
MENTAL INSIDE YOU WHICH MUST
BE CAST OUT WHICH COMPETES
FOR YOUR NAME AND SHALL OUT-
LAST YOU FOR ETERNITY YOU
MUST EXCISE IT FOR IT IS A LEECH.

XVIII

Alberta was my next destination. This was my first international dig. I acquired a passport, but this was the only time I had intended to travel out of the country for some time at least.

I felt reinvigorated.

This time around I would be dispatched to the Sulphur Mountain Formation in the western extremity of the province. Primarily siltstone, it is dated to be Early to Middle Triassic in age. The formation has yielded primarily marine life, including fish and marine reptiles. Of the marine reptiles found there, they are mostly thalattosaurs, but there have been ichthyosaur remains found as well. The Sulphur Mountain Formation is also used to harvest building stone.

Due to its close proximity to the Athabasca tar sands, Alberta is a producer of crude oil. While it operates under a humid-continental climate, there are a variety of biomes in the region, from taiga to prairie, with diverse flora and fauna occupying these habitats. Aside from the Sulphur Mountain Formation, Alberta bears some of the most Late Cretaceous dinosaur fossils in the West. *Albertosaurus*, a tyrannosaur, was discovered in the province in 1910 by the legendary American paleontologist Barnum Brown. The recently-discovered *Borealpelta*, that Cretaceous gargoyle, was also a type specimen from the province. Trace fossils, like the Grande Cache Trackways, are likewise an important find in Alberta.

I flew to Alberta to meet with the others at the university.

There was Jeffrey Maddox, head of the geological sciences department. His moustache was comb-shaped and his hair was grey as a cloudy sky. He was obese, but assured that he was fit for the trip. I had done this for years, he said, my body won't fail me now; being a paleontologist is more satisfying on the bones than bodybuilding, which I used to be, but cannot take it anymore, so I got fat, though I can still move around just fine; climbing might be an issue, though. Jeffrey's main area of study was *Pachyrhinosaurus*, which is a type species in Alberta.

There was Francois Lorrain, a Quebec native and transfer from the Université de Montréal, who was fluent in both French and English. His accent was thick, but it was not difficult to understand him. Francois was fair yet bold in the face, lacked spectacles, and had facial hair which reminded me of Georges Perec. He wouldn't disclose his area of study to us, since he was an undergraduate and still had time to discover.

There was Leslie Murdoc, the most conventionally attractive addition to the team. She was built like a pornstar, I will leave it at that. If I weren't bound by professionalism she would be in my bed, tied up, pissed on. There are times when I hate my sexuality, but specimens like her makes me forget all the fear. Her specialty was ichnofossils hewn by trilobites.

There was Wanda Powell, the least conventionally attractive addition to the team. She was not an individual who aged like wine, but rather like milk. Wanda was undoubtedly the most feeble individual on the dig; it was only a matter of time before she would be restricted to a walker and condemned to a nursing home. She really ought to have stayed behind. I don't remember what her specialty was.

There was Caleb Grant, who was, aesthetically speaking, an unremarkable stoner. I was stuck with him and Jeffrey in the caravan. I don't know whether or not he brought weed along with him. I didn't ask, but if he did say yes, I would not have bummed any from him, as smoking does nothing for me. Caleb had a fake jellyfish pendant on at all times, brandishing it with pride as if it were a cross. I believe he was more of a generalist than a specialist.

We drove along the clear Spray River and admired the infestation of wildflowers from the highway. The impressive mountains clawed the sky. The grass was flushed with a dark green. It was one of the most scenic drives I've ever been on; a banquet for the senses, arousing the primordial tourist urge inside me. I took copious amounts of photographs. I usually don't on digs. I am not one to be sentimental.

Though we were digging in its namesake, we never saw Sulphur Mountain up close. It is a national park, so excavating at that location is prohibited by Canadian law. There are, apparently, a couple of hot springs on the slopes of the mountain for commercial use.

The presence of hot springs on Sulphur Mountain made me remember when I went to Big Bone Lick State Park in Kentucky shortly after I read *Big Bone Lick: Cradle of American Paleontology* by Stanley Hedeen (University of Kentucky Press, 2008) as a sort of pilgrimage. The site was, in conjunction with Siberia, where the first mastodon and mammoth fossils were found. The native population interpreted mammoth tusks as the horns of a race of godly bison, and, until the efforts of French anatomist Georges Cuvier demonstrated that they were indeed tusks from a novel type of elephant, so did the white men. It could be argued that the very concept of extinction originated in bumfuck Kentucky. An array of other mammals have been found at the site, including elk and the ground sloth *Megalonyx jeffersonii* named after President Thomas Jefferson. Though *Megalonyx jeffersonii* was initially discovered in Greenbrier County, West Virginia (indeed, it had been christened the state fossil by Governor Joe Manchin in 2008), Big Bone Lick prides itself for having this animal in its repertoire. Jefferson himself, when he commissioned Lewis and Clark to chart the land acquired from the Louisiana Purchase, believed that ground sloths still roamed the plains of the West.

I like to imagine how much that terrified him, such indescribable beasts lumbering about like the Titans before them, performing their business unmolested and uncontested. The unknown—the greatest anxiety of mankind. Take death. We all die; there are objective things that happen following death; *rigor mortis*, decay, etc.; but again, the Big Black is uncharted, even though it takes us all; it is like asking a fish to map the ocean; it is ironic that foreigners to the water have charted it; so foreigners will have to chart our death, whether that be alien or angel.

We made camp.

At dawn we set forth towards the mountains. The outcrops lay naked against the sunrise, waiting to be plundered, pirates we are. I did not disclose my paranoia to the team. They would think I am crazy, as everyone else did. We softened our pace to accommodate Leslie.

The mountains were not difficult to climb, and Leslie agreed.

"Why did marine reptiles go extinct?" Caleb asked.

"Well, for the mosasaurs and plesiosaurs at least," I interjected, "the asteroid of the K-T boundary finished them. As for the the ichthyosaurs, I remember a study by Fischer et al in *Nature* which claimed that increased environmental volatility and diminished diversity contributed to their demise. Fuck-all is known about pliosaurs."

"Damn. We really should have brought an expert in marine reptiles on board, since this place is known for yielding those."

"There aren't many people in the field that focus on them."

"Wonder why? They're fucking fascinating, bro."

"Yeah," Jeffrey agreed. "They're underrated animals."

"Some of the most striking beasts to ever live," Francois said.

"Well said, Francois," Leslie remarked.

We scoured until late afternoon. Nothing.

Again the next day. Nothing.

Nothing.

Conodonts.

Nothing.

A brachiopod.

Nothing.

Something remarkable.

A tooth from a marine reptile!

"This is why I live," I said.

"This is why all of us live," Francois said.

"Imbued in this tooth," Jeffrey said, "is the meaning of life."

We clapped.

Again the next day. Nothing.

Nothing.

Fucking god.

This cannot be real.

It was an ungulate. Fully preserved. Triassic.

Six legs.

They acknowledged it.

I was not crazy.

We excavated for weeks. There was static in the air. Mammals this advanced in the Triassic! Mutant body plan!

We also photographed.

This was the crowning moment of my career. *Pyknosaurus* has been eclipsed.

If this happens once more I am going to kill myself.

The photographs we took of the ungulate were invariably corrupted. The photos looked like scrambled pornography. We took them with high-dollar cameras, so it is inexplicable as to why this happened. It was not especially humid in Alberta, nor was the camera molested in any way. The manner in which we took the photographs was procedural. Additionally, the photos I took of the scenery developed flawlessly.

If this happens once more I am going to kill myself.

The remains of the ungulate disappeared. We stored them in marked crates and stored them in a conspicuous location. They were stolen, perhaps, but I don't think so. They simply vanished, aborted from existence.

If this happens once more I am going to kill myself.

The team had amnesia of the dig. I interrogated everyone. They denied ever having been to Alberta at the appointed time. They called me a crazy cunt. Jeffrey Maddox even threatened to report me to the museum. I begged him not to. He complied, but the threat itself was enough to paralyze me.

If this happens once more I am going to kill myself.

XIX

Therefore I am losing my mind.
Therefore I am losing my mind.
Therefore I am losing my mind.

But what of you?
But what of you?
But what of you?
But what of you?

Therefore I am fine.
Therefore I am fine.
Therefore I am fine.
Therefore I am fine.

And you are, too.

And you are, too.

Cogito ergo sum.

Cogitas ergo es.

Cogito ergo non sum.

Cogitas ergo nonne tu es.

XX

This would be my last dig.

I was going out west, the badlands; the iconic landscape that every paleontologist dreams of working in.

It was out west where Edward Drinker Cope and Othniel Charles Marsh had their infamous war over dinosaur bones. It was out west where we found out that America was partially submerged in a shallow sea during the Mesozoic. It was out west where *Tyrannosaurus* was discovered.

The American West is the cradle of paleontology as it is understood by laymen.

I was going to Hell Creek in Montana. I had not been there before. This would be an experience.

Vincent Rosenbaum and Garrett Young would accompany me.

The others were from The University of Boulder and The University of Denver.

Marcus Gormeister, from Boulder, a grad student.

Tyler Joyce, from Denver, a professor of the geology department, specializing in sedimentology.

Hannah Siler, from Dever, a grad student.

Aside from my colleagues at the museum, I don't remember their faces.

I am ashamed of that.

We departed for the badlands in early spring when the temperature was serene.

It was an arduous flight and an arduous drive.

What were we looking for? Whatever presented itself. What diverse fossiliferous rocks are present!

It was like wading through a dream.

The rocks were naked and the vegetation was short and scarce. It was not quite a desert.

※

On the first day we trekked for hours.
I was growing thirsty
And my feet were growing blistered.
"I am tired," I said.
"We've just got a little more to go," they said.
I said, they said, I don't remember.
This went on for a half-hour.
Or was it an hour?
Then I saw it.
There was no rhyme to it.
There was no meter to it.
There was no reason to it.
It was more insane than *Opabinia*.
Than *Hallucigenia*.
Than *Wiwaxia*.
It was non-Euclidean.
It was not of this earth, yet of this earth.
It was an hallucination.
It was the death of hallucination.
It was the birth of reason.
It churned like a cauldron.
It hissed like a serpent.

The manner of fossilization was unlike anything anyone had ever encountered.
I screamed at the top of my lungs.
I blacked out.
Then at the crest of my vision was a light.
A light.
I plummeted towards the light.
The light seared my retinas.
I found myself somewhere else.
Away from the badlands.
Away from my colleagues.
Away from everything earthly.
The biology was uncanny.
The atmosphere was fierce and eldritch.
I was an anachronism.
I saw creatures I studied approach me.
The creatures that they denied.
There was no regard for time here.
This is what divorces me from biologists.
I cannot handle the living.
The living repulse me.
I fled them.
The landscape bent beneath my feet.
The space around me contorted.

The time around me shivered.
I saw the Six.
First, Ordovician.
Second, Devonian.
Third, Permian.
Fourth, Triassic.
Fifth, Cretaceous.
Sixth, Anthropocene.
I saw all the creatures I loved go away.
I saw all the creatures I hated survive.
The birth of the moon.
The death of the sun.
The universe in an epileptic fit.
The spacetime contortions ceased.
I was in the back room of the museum.
My colleagues.
All of them.
They began to embrace me, one by one.
They apologized.
They got on their knees and prayed to me.
They took out whips.
They flagellated themselves.
Drops of blood flew everywhere.
Spacetime whisked me away.

Fossilization in real-time.

The death of a beautiful dinosaur.

Nature cannot stand the sight of it.

It is buried.

Three-way potential.

Permineralization.

Replacement.

Recrystallization.

You decide.

I discover it millions of years later.

It is *Pyknosaurus*.

When I unearthed it, it rearticulated itself from the stones.

It regenerated bone.

Tissue.

Muscle.

Flesh.

Pyknosaurus was the Christ.

Pyknosaurus mocked me.

YOU DO NOT KNOW MY TRUE NAME.

YOU WILL NEVER KNOW MY TRUE NAME.

WHAT AUTHORITY DO YOU HAVE TO NAME ME?

ONLY ADAM HAS THAT AUTHORITY.
I came to.
Still screaming.
I was restrained.
They knocked me out, unsure of what else to do.

XXI

They did not see what I saw.

This is a blessing, for they know I am not insane.

Science is futile. All of the knowledge we will ever accumulate will be incomplete and temporary. I will not be satiated. I can never be satiated. I want to know everything. This is why I joined the sciences, to know more than the lay, to be a citizen of humanity.

But I know now that this was for naught.

This is my greatest solace.

My life was for nothing.

I will die a virgin.

XXII

(The following poem was found next to the body of D.W. Lambert, some days after she committed suicide by overdosing on sleeping pills.)

The beginning of time
Leading up to this moment;
This moment leading up to
The end of time.

The words on this page
Will die with me,
Like the syllables
On your tongue.

This is pointless,
Like a sickness,

Like breathing,
Like eating.

I yearn to see
The boat of Charon
To suck me in
And bear me away.

A PARTIAL LIST OF SNUGGLY BOOKS

CPSIA information can be obtained
at www.ICGtesting.com
Printed in the USA
LVHW051443060222
710279LV00003B/204